Dear
Gigi
+
Olive...

May your worlds be
filled with magical stori[es]

♡ Stephanie
Sorkin

"Wouldn't the world be a boring
place if we were all the same?"

—Stephanie Sorkin

www.mascotbooks.com

For more information, please contact:
Mascot Books
620 Herndon Parkway, Suite 320
Herndon, VA 20170
info@mascotbooks.com

Library of Congress Control Number: 2020900371

CPSIA Code: PRTWP0720A
ISBN-13: 978-1-64543-294-4

Printed in South Korea

Am I a UNICORN?

Stephanie Sorkin

Illustrated by
Srimalie Bassani

I am never surprised at students' reactions when I ask them to describe their YOUniform. Without fail, one by one, they will look down at their clothes and peek around the room to see what their classmates are wearing. How rewarding it is for me, as an educator, to teach a valuable lesson with a simple play on words.

"No two YOUniforms are alike," I explain.

"But uniforms are all the same!" is the usual reply.

"We don't wear uniforms to school," is another.

Now, the lesson:

Your YOUniform has nothing to do with how you are dressed. It's about the little, individual pieces ON THE INSIDE that make you an original, YOUnique human being.

Your personality, creativity, determination, and courage.

Your imagination, talents, heart, and mind.

Everything added all together, piece by piece, to make you...YOU!!
Congrats on being one of a kind!

It all starts out as a regular day.
I get up, brush my teeth...
And even put some toys away.

But there is something I missed,
Laying right on the stairs.
A teddy bear, my favorite,
with brown, curly hair.

So when mom yells "breakfast"
(She's amazing at cooking),
I just run down the stairs
without even looking.
I trip and I slip,
It all happens so fast!
BOOM! That's my head!
Are those stars flying past?
Now my mom dashes over
After hearing the fall.
I look up from the ground,
Is she always this tall?
Her face looks sort of strange,
Like she's kind of surprised.
Something must be wrong!
I can see it in her eyes!

"I think I'll be fine, Mom.
I'm feeling alright."
"Your horn's gone!" Mom screams.
"It's nowhere in sight!"

My horn, did she say?
Did I hear the words right?
The thing that glows brightly
When day turns to night?

My beautiful horn that makes me,
well, me?
Broke off just like that?
How could it be?

Soon, my dog finds the horn
Right under the couch.
Grabs it tight with his teeth,
I want to say OUCH!
But I CAN'T FEEL IT
Because it's NOT ON MY HEAD!!!
Am I still a *UNICORN?!*
I wonder with dread.

My mom takes me by the leg
And leads me outside.
"We have to get this fixed.
We're going for a ride."

Just then, I see it...

"WE FIX HORNS" it says on the sign.

So I rush in and move to the front of the line.

"It's an emergency, please help! My horn is broken."

The mechanic laughed and said, "You must be jokin'."

"No, sir, I'm serious. I'm a UNICORN, you see?"

I beg and I plead.

I need my horn to be ME!

"Listen buddy," he shouts, "I hope you can hear!

We fix horns in CARS, not horns on HEADS!

Do I make myself clear?"

If they won't fix it
I'll do it myself!
I run home to my closet
Pulling things off the shelf.
Glue, string, and tape,
That'll do the trick.
I'll try all three
Until one helps it stick!
A little of this
and a little of that.
Thought this would
hold it on,
but it's still falling flat.

I'm trying again,
This time, I'll use more.
But it still doesn't work...
It falls right on the floor!

Tomorrow comes fast
And my horn's still not there.
Just a stump on my head
Growing out of my hair!
Of all times to be HORNLESS,
Today's NOT the day!
I'm the special guest at a party
For a little girl's birthday.

She's expecting a UNICORN,
The kind she's seen before.
So I'm feeling very nervous
walking up to the door.

"No, you're a horse!!!
With those hooves on your feet?
Should we get you a saddle
And some carrots to eat?"
"Whatever you are,
you sure don't have a horn!"
Then they all say it together:
"YOU'RE NOT A UNICORN!"
The group bursts into laughter.
There is no end in sight.
It takes all of my courage
And all of my might!
"Please, everyone!" I say,
"Would you listen to me?
I AM a UNICORN!
I'll prove it,
Just wait and see!"

"when I sneeze it's gold glitter!
AAACCCHHHHOOOO!
That's for you!"

"When my belly gets gassy,
Welp, here it goes.
It smells like cotton candy,
No need to hold your nose!"

"I believe in miracles,
rainbows and magic too.
I believe in dreams and sparkles,
and all that UNICORNS do.
But most of all, I have a heart
that's made of pure gold.
That's more important for a
UNICORN than any horn
can behold."

At this moment, it hits me
with my eyes open wide.
It's what I feel in my soul,
what's on the INSIDE!
"I don't need a horn
To make me, well, ME.
I'm as much of a UNICORN
As I ever will be!"

"You're one of a kind," says a tiny voice.
"Just perfect. It's true.
I believe in UNICORNS," says the birthday girl.
"I believe in you."

Classroom Discussion Questions

1. What is the overall lesson of the story?

2. What was the UNICORN'S mistake? Why did they fall down the stairs?

3. Why does the UNICORN attempt to get their horn fixed?

4. What is your YOUniform? What are five characteristics that make you who you are?

5. Was it okay that the other animals teased the UNICORN for not having a horn?

6. Why did the UNICORN misunderstand the sign that read "WE FIX HORNS"?

7. What are the emotions that the UNICORN is feeling when they walk into the birthday party?

8. When we make friends, what qualities do you think are more important? The ones on the inside, outside, or both?

9. Will it be possible for the UNICORN to forgive the other animals?

10. What will you do in the future if you see someone being teased for their differences?

YOUnique Rainbow Cupcakes

Every cupcake is different. How beautiful is that?

Cupcakes

- ☆ 1 cup (2 sticks) of softened butter
- ☆ 1 cup sugar
- ☆ 2 cups flour
- ☆ 1 tsp baking powder
- ☆ 3 eggs
- ☆ 1 tsp vanilla extract
- ☆ Assorted food coloring

Directions:

1. Preheat oven to 350 degrees Fahrenheit.
2. Mix butter, vanilla extract, and eggs with an electric mixer.
3. Slowly add the sugar, flour, and baking powder. Mix until smooth.
4. Separate batter into five bowls. Add different colored food coloring, one color to each bowl.
5. Add a spoonful of each color batter to a lined cupcake tin. All five colors should be in each tin. This will create a rainbow effect once baked.
6. Bake for 15-20 minutes.
7. Let cool for 15 minutes.

Vanilla Frosting

- ☆ 4 cups confectioners' sugar
- ☆ 4 tbsp butter, softened
- ☆ 4 tbsp milk
- ☆ 1 tsp vanilla extract

Directions:

Combine sugar, butter, milk, and vanilla.
Beat on medium speed until light and fluffy.

Want to add to the fun?

Sprinkle sparkly glitter sugar in the color of your choice or add rainbow colored candy on top for extra smiles!

Food Allergies?

This recipe can be easily adjusted to fit your needs!

- ★ For gluten-free treats, use gluten-free flour.
- ★ For an egg-free option, substitute the eggs with one 6 ounce container of Greek yogurt.
- ★ For a dairy-free option, use Parve, non-dairy margarine in place of the butter and a dairy-free alternative for the milk. This recipe is peanut and tree-nut free, assuming that you check the manufacturing practices of all the ingredients.

Need to save time?

Use your favorite cake mix and follow the directions on the box...
then simply follow the steps to make it full of color!

ENJOY!!

About the Author

Stephanie Sorkin lives in New York with her husband and three kids. She is the author of the award winning books *Nutley, the Nut-Free Squirrel, Chocolate Shoes with Licorice Laces* and *Frenemy Jane, the Sometimes Friend.* A portion of the proceeds from all of her books are donated to charities that benefit children.

Stephanie is a member of SCBWI and LICWI, and spends her time visiting schools to discuss the writing process and the joys of creativity.

For more information, please visit StephanieSorkin.com.